This book belongs to

....

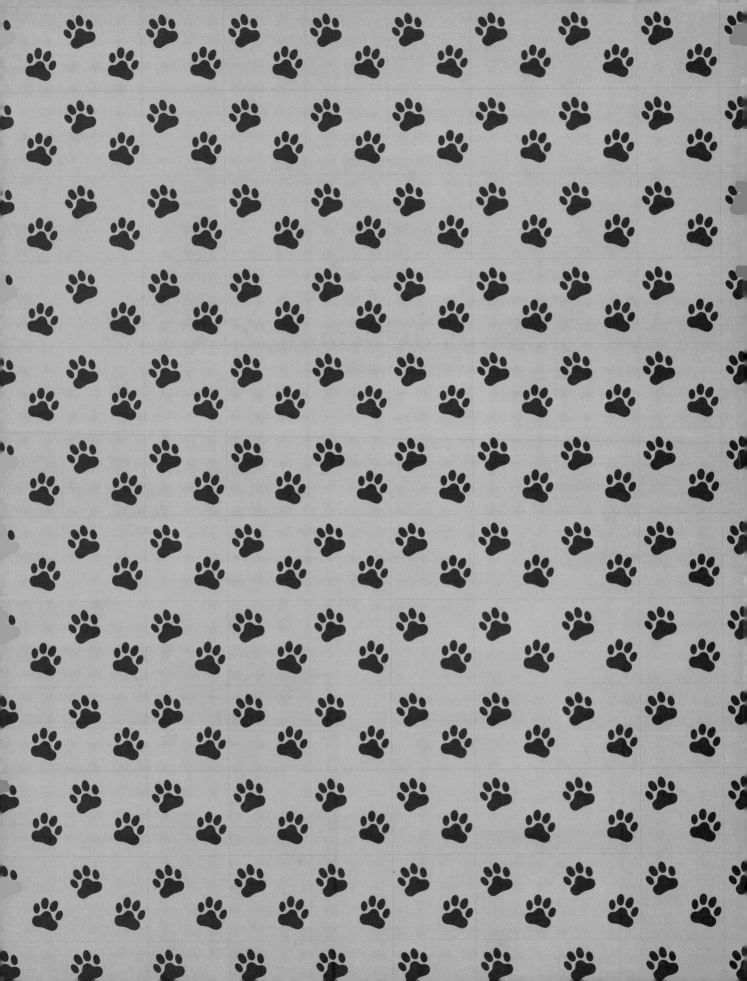

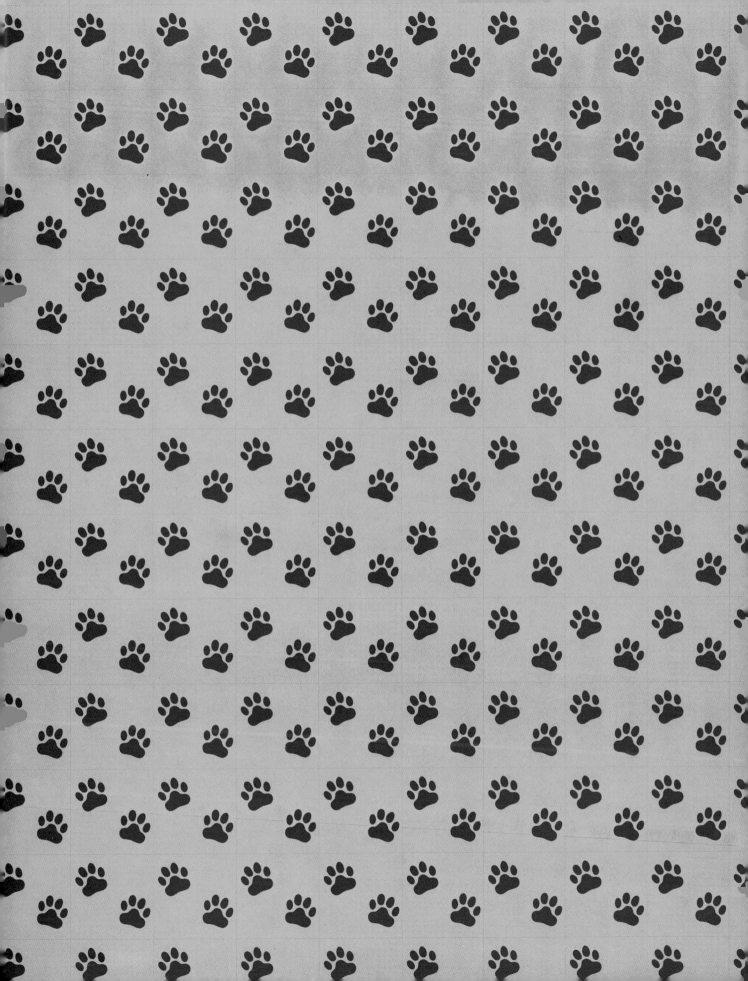

This edition first published in 2018 by Alligator Products Ltd
Cupcake is an imprint of Alligator Products Ltd,
2nd Floor, 314 Regents Park Road, London, N3 2JX
www.alligatorbooks.co.uk

Copyright © 2018 Alligator Products Ltd
Written by Christine Swift
Illustrated by Claire Stimpson

Printed in China.0811

Mummy knows best

Written by Christine Swift
Illustrated by Claire Stimpson

cupcake

Tommy loved to play chase and hide-and-seek on the grassland.

Playing with his friends was so much fun...

but there were lots of bushes and prickly thorns.

"Ouch!" cried Tommy, as a thorn hurt his paw.

Tommy wanted to stay and play
with his friends.

His paw was really hurting now though.

"Come on Tommy, you need to rest your paw",
said his mummy.

"But I want to play!" cried Tommy.

Soon his paw hurt even more!

Tommy started to cry.

Tommy felt very sad. His friends were having so much fun playing hide-and-seek. He wanted to join in.

"With a little rest it will get better" said his mummy,
as she gave him a cuddle.

As Tommy went to bed that night, he felt sad that he had missed all the fun.

"Don't be sad", said his mummy,
"If you rest it will get better".

Tommy soon fell fast asleep.

Sure enough, the next day, Tommy awoke
and his foot was better.

"Thank you mummy," said Tommy,
"You were right!"

Tommy raced off to play with his friends, happy that he had listened to his Mummy.

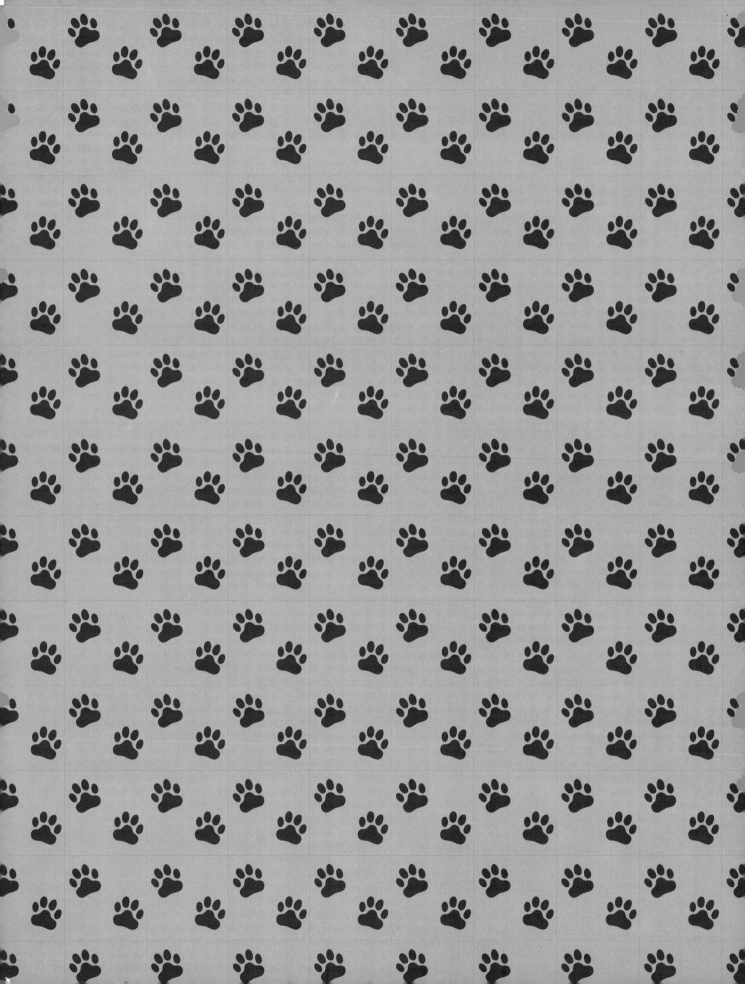

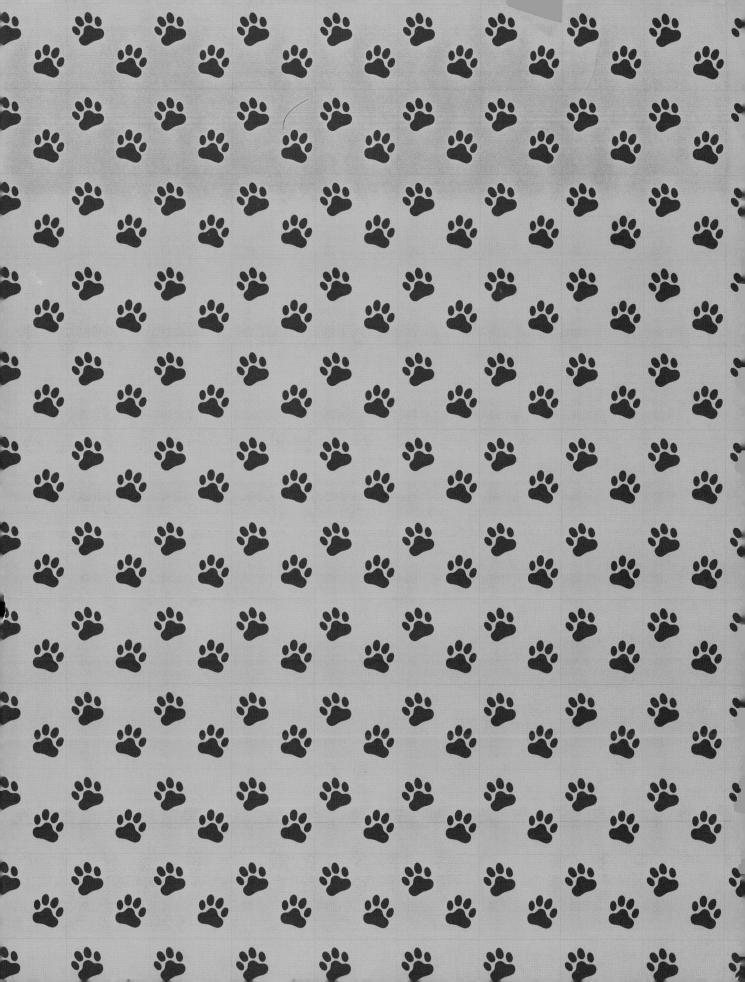